DATE DUE

MAY 30 2001		JUL 02 2008	
DEC 23 2001			
AUG 23 2006			

To Dizi, with love

—M. C. B. and T. W.

Henry Holt and Company, Inc.
Publishers since 1866
115 West 18th Street
New York, New York 10011

Published in Canada by Fitzhenry & Whiteside Ltd.,
195 Allstate Parkway, Markham, Ontario L3R 4T8.

Library of Congress Cataloging-in-Publication Data
Brusca, María Cristina.
When jaguars ate the moon, and other stories about animals and plants
of the Americas / retold by María Cristina Brusca and Tona Wilson.
1. Indians—Folklore. 2. Tales—America. 3. Plants—America—Folklore.
4. Animals—America—Folklore. I. Wilson, Tona. II. Title.
E59.F6B78 1994 398.24'097—dc20 93-50197

ISBN 0-8050-2797-1

First Edition—1995

Printed in the United States of America
on acid-free paper.∞

1 3 5 7 9 10 8 6 4 2

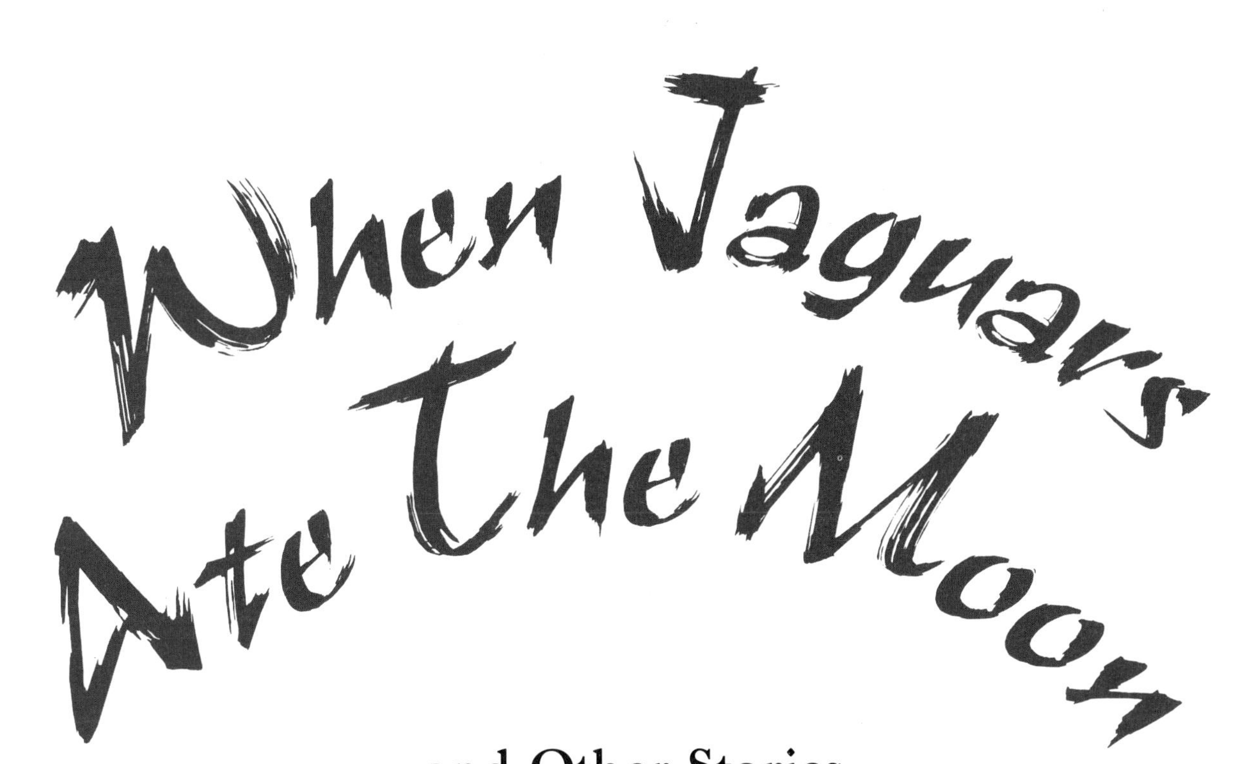

and Other Stories
About Animals and Plants
of the Americas

Retold by
María Cristina Brusca and Tona Wilson

Illustrated by
María Cristina Brusca

Henry Holt and Company
New York

From Anteater to Zompopo

Why anteater? And *why* zompopo? And what *is* a zompopo anyway? A zompopo is a leaf-cutter ant. And anteaters eat ants.

What else do the zompopo and the anteater have to do with each other? Both come from the Americas, and both appear in stories told by people who have lived on these continents for tens of thousands of years.

This is a book of plants and animals of the Americas, and of stories about them. They are arranged from A to Z, with more than a hundred of these plants and animals presented at the tops of the pages. And there is at least one story for each letter of the English alphabet. Some of these are our retellings of anecdotes and very short stories; others grew from scraps of longer stories. Most are part of oral traditions and have been handed down for generations. In a few cases we have retold short episodes from ancient myths that were set down in writing hundreds of years ago.

When the Europeans first arrived in what they

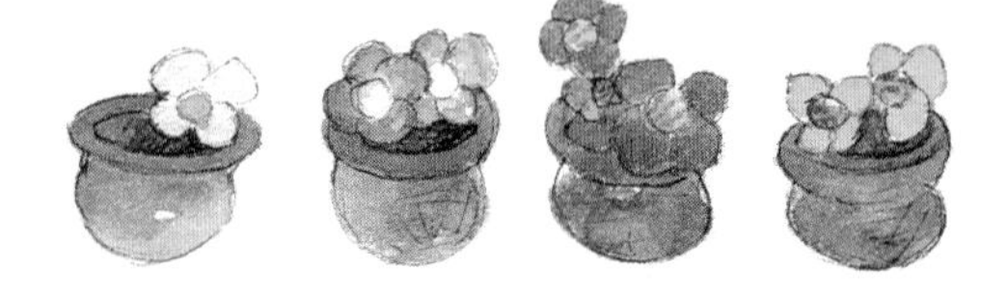

called the "new world," they found many plants and animals they had never seen before. They drew pictures of them, wrote about them, and carried them back to Europe to present to their kings and queens.

But for the people who already lived here, "exotic" creatures like the anteater were the familiar animals they hunted, feared, or found amusing. And the people had cultivated food plants like corn, which was unknown to the Europeans, for thousands of years.

So just as European myths and folktales told of horses, storks, and cabbage, those of the "new world" spoke of llamas, hummingbirds, and corn. The stories in this book are not identical to the ones told five hundred years ago. Oral traditions are always changing, and those of a colonized land are particularly fragile: many have been lost or hidden under other tales "imported" from Europe. But we have tried to include stories whose central motifs come from the Americas.

Today, some of these animals and plants, like the potato, are known all over the world. Others, like the tapir, still seem "exotic" to many people. Still others, like the auk, have become extinct or, like the kinkajou, are threatened with extinction.

The threat is not limited to plants and animals. Their disappearance—together with many other factors—has meant disaster for the people who first told the stories in this book.

The animals that are extinct will not return. Nor will cultures that have been destroyed.

We can, however, hope that the destruction stops right now. We can listen to each other's stories and find that plants and animals frighten, touch, or amuse us in many of the same ways they have frightened, touched, and amused human beings for thousands and thousands of years.

Anteater

Armadillo

Avocado

The Anteater: Origin of the Dance

A long, long time ago, a man and an animal were searching for food in the forest. The animal waddled along on all fours, looking for ants to eat. The man followed; the anteater seemed to him an easy catch.

He raised his club high in the air and was about to bring it down. Suddenly the anteater reared up on its hind legs! It staggered toward the hunter, threatening him with its front claws. Again and again he tried to hit the animal with his club, but each time it tottered out of his reach. Finally the man got so dizzy that he dropped his club and fell to the ground. The anteater waddled off into the forest.

"Didn't you catch anything?" asked the hunter's friends when he came home empty-handed. The man shook his head. "I almost got an anteater, but when I raised my club, it stood up like this . . ." And the man staggered around the fire waving his arms. His friends laughed. Soon they were all wobbling around the fire waving their arms and laughing about the anteater that got away. And that is how the Guaraní people learned to dance.

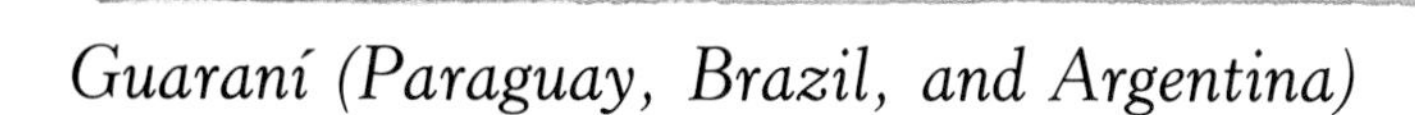

Guaraní (Paraguay, Brazil, and Argentina)

Alligator

Agouti

Anaconda

How the Armadillo Got Its Armor

When the world was new, the animals had no feathers, no scales, no furry coats—just their skins. But each animal did have a loom. So one day they all sat down to make themselves some clothes. The puma wove herself a golden suit, the skunk a black-and-white cape, and the lizard a gleaming leotard.

The armadillo sat down to weave too. He worked neatly at first, but soon he began to daydream, and his weaving became loose and sloppy. The other animals teased him. "What a messy poncho!" they snickered.

The armadillo felt so ashamed that he couldn't look his friends in the eye. Without saying anything, or even fixing the loose part of his poncho, he wove the rest extra tight. When he finished, the poncho was narrow at each end and wide in the middle. And when the armadillo put it on, it hardened around him like a suit of armor.

In the northwest of Argentina, some people say this was a punishment for his sloppy weaving. But when the armadillo is frightened, it seems more like a reward: After all, what other animal can curl itself into a tight armored ball and roll away?

Northwestern Argentina

B

Beans

Buffalo

Beaver

The Beans

Mayan rain spirits live in mountain caves. To make the peoples' crops grow, the spirits go to their pots of thunder, lightning, rain, and wind, and measure out just the right amount of each ingredient. When they get angry they make floods or droughts.

The rain spirits carried a man off to their cave to help them out. But he couldn't learn to make rain. When the crops were dry and a good soaking rain was needed, he timidly measured out a little drizzle. The next time, he opened all the pots at once, and made a terrible storm.

Finally, the spirits made him their cook. They very carefully measured out some beans for him in a pot, just the right amount. Then they went out to make rain. The man looked into the pot. "Not enough beans," he thought. So he put in another handful. And then another, and another . . .

The water boiled. The beans grew. They spilled over the sides of the pot, onto the floor, out the mouth of the cave, and down the mountain! "It's time for you to go home!" the spirits told the man. But they liked him. After that, his crops always got just the right amount of rain.

Maya (Guatemala and Mexico)

Coyote

Condor

Capybara

Coyote and the Origin of Death

The Caddo people of North America tell of a time when nobody died. The world got so crowded that there wasn't enough food for everybody. So the animal people had a meeting to decide what to do.

Someone suggested that people could die for a short time, and then, after a little rest, come back to life. Everybody liked that idea, except for Coyote. "We'd still run out of food. People should die forever," he argued.

But everyone else agreed that dying forever would be too sad. "Okay," said Coyote, but he wasn't really satisfied.

Soon somebody died. After letting the dead person's spirit rest for a few months, the shamans went to a special grass house and sang to let the spirit know it was time to come back.

When the shamans had been singing for many days, a whirlwind came blowing toward them. The dead person's spirit was inside it! Just as the whirlwind reached the grass house, Coyote closed the door. The spirit, seeing itself shut out, swept by the house and disappeared into the distance.

Ever since that time, people have died forever, and Coyote has been an outcast. The other people beat him and chased him away. He still looks back over each shoulder to see if anyone is following him.

Caddo (formerly Texas and Arkansas; later Oklahoma)

Corn

Corn and Chocolate

The gods of ancient Mexico created people, and then they had to find something for them to eat.

Quetzalcoatl, the plumed serpent god, looked around and saw a red ant carrying a kernel of corn. "Where did you get that?" he asked the ant, but she didn't answer. Again and again he asked, until finally the ant told him to come with her.

Turning himself into a black ant, Quetzalcoatl followed the red ant to the Food Mountain, where all the corn, beans, peppers, and other foods were hidden. Together the two ants carried corn to the other gods, who chewed it for the new people and placed it on their lips to strengthen them.

The people needed to be able to get the corn, so one of the gods split the mountain open. But the rain gods got to the food before anyone else and stole it. After that, they gave people just a little food each year, and only in return for human sacrifice.

Aztec (Mexico)

• • •

Quetzalcoatl took many forms. At one time he lived on earth as a man and became the leader of the Toltec people.

Under Quetzalcoatl's leadership, the Toltecs grew huge vegetables: the squashes were six feet around, and each ear of corn had to be carried with both arms. Cotton grew in red, green, blue, violet, and all the other colors; it never had to be dyed.

The land was covered with flowering cacao trees. The Toltecs roasted and ground the cacao beans and mixed them with water. They sweetened this with honey and flavored it with vanilla and flower petals to make "the drink of the gods." And they called it *chocolatl.*

ruddy Duck

Dogwood

white-tailed Deer

Big Duck and the Ducks

There was once a lazy man named Twentgowa, which means Big Duck. He didn't hunt. He just slept all day. "Your children have nothing to eat but corn bread," said his wife, "and you sit around like a duck on its nest!"

Twentgowa went out into the forest. There he met a mysterious stranger, who dove into the water and caught a lot of ducks just by tying their feet together. Twentgowa wanted to learn to do that too.

So the stranger taught him, and gave him magic cords. "But," he warned, "you may use this food-getting magic only twice. No more!"

Twentgowa tried the magic and caught three ducks. He tossed them back into the water. Then he thanked the stranger and started home.

On his way, he passed a lake filled with ducks. "I'd better try out my magic," he thought. "What if it works only when I'm with the stranger?"

So Twentgowa dove into the water and caught five ducks. He threw them back into the water and hurried home.

"I have food-getting magic," he told his wife. "Watch!" He dove into the duck pond and tied all of the ducks' feet together. But he had used up his magic. The ducks all flapped their wings. They rose out of the water and flew high into the sky, with Twentgowa dangling from his magic cords, screaming . . . until the cords broke and he went tumbling into a hollow stump. The ducks flew on, glad to be free of that silly Big Duck, who had tried to catch them with magic.

Seneca (northern New York State)

Emperor penguin

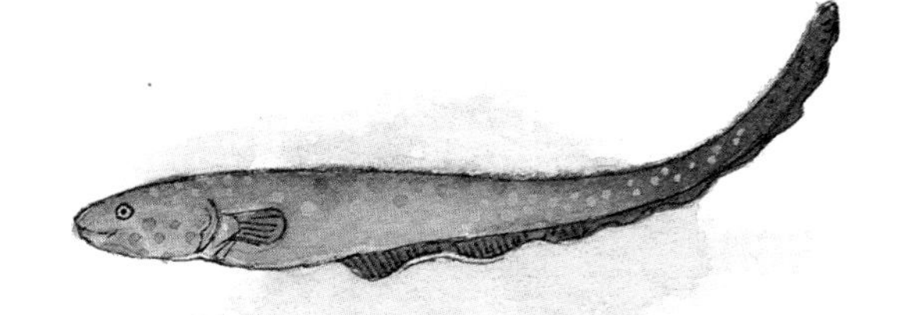

Electric Eel

bald Eagle

Where Emperor Penguins Come From

The Selk'nam are gone now. But they, like the Caddo, told of a time when people didn't die. They just went to sleep for a while and woke up refreshed. Sometimes, after many lives, people got tired of being human and became rocks, clouds, mountains, or penguins.

Time passed, and a big flood covered the whole world, and people were floundering around in the cold water. Some of them climbed up onto the ice floes and joined the penguins. They ate fish and played in the icy water, and, as time passed, they turned into great big penguins.

When the water went down again, some people went back to living on land as humans. But others were happy to stay out on the ice. Now they are emperor penguins. They spend most of their lives on the ice floes and almost never come to shore.

Selk'nam (now extinct) and Yamana (both southern tip of Argentina)

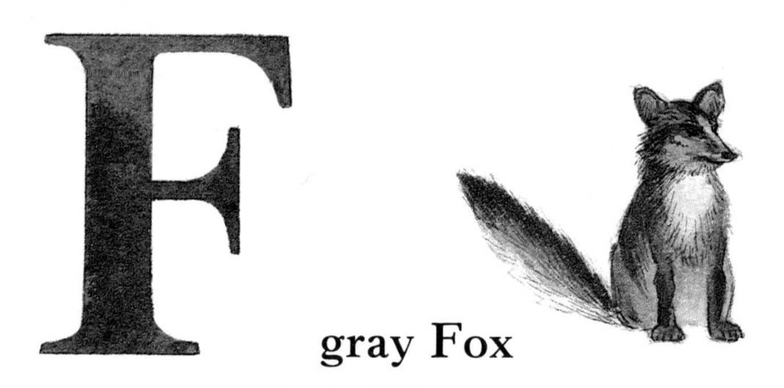

F

gray Fox

Flamingo

golden arrow poison Frog

The Singing Fox

No tropical animals live in Patagonia, the land of the Aonik'enk. But things might have been different. When Elal, the creator, finished making the turkey, the puma, the fox, and the rest of the animals, he put them all into one huge corral. The animals were so tired that they went to sleep right away.

The next morning the fox woke up before anyone else and began to sing loudly to greet the rising sun. He had an awful voice that jolted the other animals from their slumber. The other animals leapt up in terror. Without stopping to find out what was causing the racket, they kicked down the walls and stampeded out of the corral. And away the animals galloped, hopped, and slithered.

If the fox's singing hadn't scared them away to the north, east, and west, all the animals would have lived in the far south, in the cold and desolate Patagonia. The Aonik'enk still sing in the morning to greet the sun.

Aonik'enk (southern Argentina)

Grizzly bear 

Guava

Guinea pig

Grizzly Bear Gets Left Behind

At first there was no fire on earth. There is a story from the Pacific Northwest about how the animal people stole it from the sky people. Chickadee shot an arrow into the sky and it stuck there; then another, which stuck to the first. Chickadee kept shooting arrows until there was a ladder that stretched from the earth to the sky.

One by one, the animals climbed up the ladder. Grizzly Bear was the last one in line to go up. "There may not be anything to eat up there," he thought. "I'd better take some food with me." So he filled a big bag with all the kinds of food he liked best and began to climb up the arrow ladder.

Up and up went the big bear. Suddenly an arrow broke. Grizzly clutched at the next arrow up, but that one broke too, and Grizzly tumbled down to earth. His big bag of food fell right on top of him. And that is why Grizzly stayed home while the rest of the animals went to get fire.

Sanpoil (northern Washington State and Canada)

Hummingbird

Huckleberry

Hoatzin

The Hummingbird and the Tapir

"How did you get so big? Huh? Huh?" All day the hummingbird hovered around the tapir, asking the same question. The hummingbird was about the size of a toucan in those days, but the tapir was *huge*.

Finally the tapir was fed up. "I burned myself in a fire," she answered. "Why don't you do the same?"

"You think I should?" asked the hummingbird. "Think I should burn myself and get big like you? Huh? You think it'll work? Huh? Huh?"

"Sure it will," growled the tapir. "It'll work just fine!"

So the hummingbird gathered lots of wood. "You think this is enough? Huh?" And built an *enormous* fire. "Is it big enough yet? Huh? Huh?" He jumped into the fire. "You think I'll get bigger now? Huh?" he began. But suddenly he felt his flesh sizzling. He was shriveling, getting smaller and smaller!

Pop! Like a little spark he flew out of the fire and plunged into the river. When he came out he was tiny, just as hummingbirds are today. And they still fly around like bright little sparks from the fire.

Yanomamo (Brazil and Venezuela)

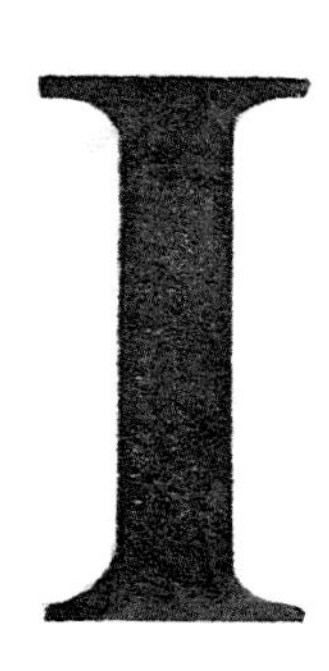

Iguana

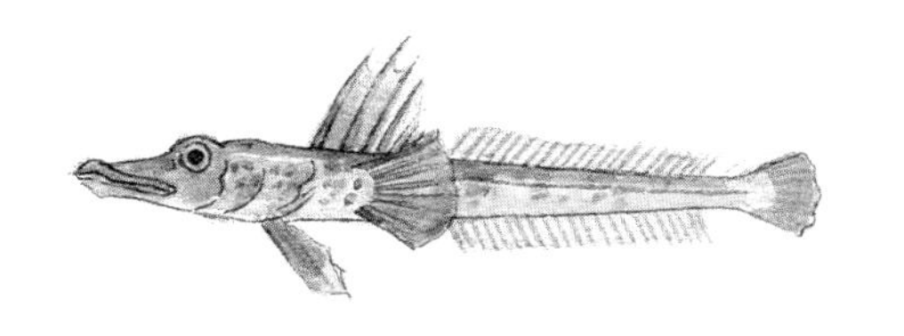

Icefish

Ibis

The First Iguana

Not very far from the Yanomamo people, who tell the story of the hummingbird, live the Cuiva. They tell of a man who wanted to camp at the very top of a tall palm tree. His friends begged him not to go. "You'll fall!" "You'll get hurt!" they all said. But the man was very stubborn. He tied his knife to a string around his forehead, to keep his hands free, and began to climb.

The people shaded their eyes and looked up as he climbed higher and higher. When he reached the very top of the tree, he waved. Then suddenly he lost his balance and plummeted down into the river. *Splash!* The man disappeared under the water.

The people waited for him to emerge, but they never saw the man again. He had turned into an iguana, the first one that ever existed.

And today's iguanas still have the habit of falling into the water from the tops of high trees, just as the first one did.

Cuiva (Colombia and Venezuela)

J

Jaguar

When Jaguars Ate the Moon

One night when everyone else was asleep, a Toba woman saw the moon bleeding! It was being eaten by jaguars! She woke her companions, and they all shouted, trying to frighten the jaguars away. They pounded their wooden mortars like drums, louder and louder.

But the jaguars weren't scared. They tore off burning chunks of the moon. Some fell into the forest, and suddenly the whole world went up in flames.

Even the rivers boiled! The water wasn't boiling in the bulrushes, so that is where some people hid. Others became animals: an old woman became an anteater. Some people and animals fled to the sky. The rhea ran so high that it became the constellation of the Southern Cross. And two dogs that ran after it became stars.

When there is an eclipse, some Toba people still make noise, yelling, shooting guns, and drumming on mortars and banging pots and pans, to keep the jaguars from eating the moon.

Toba (Paraguay, Bolivia, and northern Argentina)

K

Kinkajou

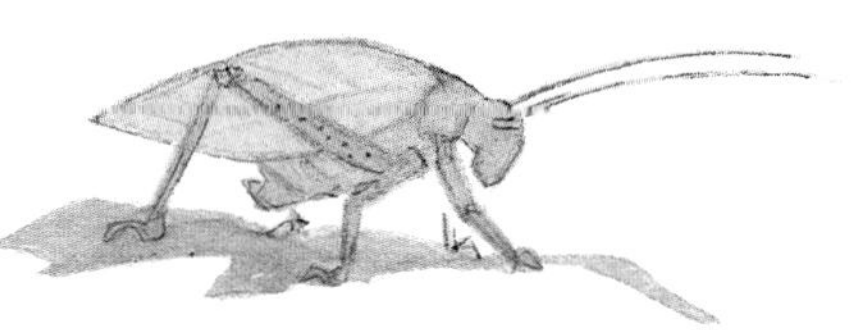

Katydid

Kangaroo rat

Kinkajou and the Food Tree

Kinkajou stayed out all night and slept all day. One morning the other animals smelled something sweet on his breath. It was not at all like mushrooms, the only food they knew.

That night, Paca followed him. She hid and watched as he climbed a tree. It was loaded with pineapples, papayas, peppers, corn, yuca, sweet potatoes, and other foods. Kinkajou bit into a pineapple, and its sweet juice dripped into Paca's mouth. She whispered, "Fall from his hand, fall down to me, fall, fall, fall down to me. . . ." And the pineapple fell into her hand! But Kinkajou saw her. He aimed another pineapple at her tail and chopped it off. Even today, her descendants are tailless.

Paca ran home to tell the other animals. Together they cut down the food tree, so everyone could eat. But Kinkajou went away to live in another part of the forest.

Cuiva (Colombia and Venezuela)

Llama

Lightning bug

Loon

The Lost Llama

One evening an Aymara shepherd was leading his llamas home through the Andes Mountains when it suddenly began to snow very hard. Fighting against the wind and blinding snow, the man finally got his llamas safely home . . . only to find that one of them was missing!

The shepherd didn't stop to rest or eat. He went back out into the storm to search for his lost llama.

The next morning it was snowing harder than ever, and the man had not returned. When, after a whole day and another night, the storm at last subsided, a search party went out to look for him.

They found the shepherd and his llama together, buried under deep snow. Both of them were dead.

But that was not the end of the llama man, or of his llama. Viracocha, the creator, revived them in the afterlife, giving the man a hundred more white llamas and a hundred black ones.

They can still be seen sometimes, on stormy days, winding their way through the Andes, not seeming to feel the cold. And when the Aymara need to find something that is lost, they still light candles to the Llama Man.

Aymara (Bolivia)

The Flood and the Howler Monkeys

With her sisters and brother, the goddess Kuma created the earth and the rivers and all the people and animals. But the first people neglected her, and Kuma became angry. She made it rain so much that only one sand dune and one tree were left above water.

Some of the people climbed up into the tree. They were safe from the water, but they had only leaves and rotten wood to eat. To make things worse, as they sat in the tree with their bottoms in the water, a big fish came swimming up under them and bit them.

Kuma spoke to them. "From now on you will live in trees, eat leaves and rotting wood, and you will forget how to talk like people."

After the flood, a few people survived as humans. They are the Yaruro, and Kuma still protects them today. But the others, the ones who climbed the tree and ate leaves and rotting wood, became howler monkeys, and are still living in the trees.

Yaruro (southwestern Venezuela)

Douroucouli
Pygmy marmoset
True marmoset
Black uakari
Callimico
Howler monkey
Tamarin
Capuchin
Spider monkey

Manatee

Moose

Macaw

The Moose and the Catfish

Once, a group of catfish decided to gang up on a moose that grazed every day at the edge of their pond. "We can ambush it, kill it with our spears, and eat it," they said.

So they hid themselves among the reeds and grass, with their spears ready. When the moose came down to the edge of the water and nibbled on the grass, the chief catfish, with all of its might, thrust a spear into the great big tough leg of the moose.

"Who has stabbed me? Why, it's a miserable catfish!" thundered the moose, and it trampled all of the catfish into the mud, killing many of them.

The ones that escaped still carry their spears. And their heads never recovered from being flattened by the moose. And that is why catfish look the way they do. A moose is not an easy animal to ambush.

Menominee (formerly Michigan and Wisconsin; now Wisconsin)

Nighthawk **Naked-backed bat** **Nutria**

The Nighthawk

A woman and her cruel husband went hunting. After a few days they were very thirsty. The man went to look for water, but he made his wife stay behind. He said he would bring her a gourd filled with water.

He found a water hole nearby and drank as much as he wanted, but he didn't fill the gourd. He told his wife he hadn't found any water.

That night the woman was too thirsty to sleep. She heard frogs croaking and knew her husband had lied: where there are frogs, there is water. She wanted to find it, but she was afraid to move.

At last, long after midnight, her head magically separated from her body and, using her hair as wings, flew away to the water hole. The man soon awoke and saw his wife's headless body. In a rage, he stamped on the glowing coals and put out the campfire.

When the woman's head tried to return to her body, the fire was gone and she couldn't find her camp. Her head became a nighthawk, with wings that were once hair fluttering and quivering as she searches endlessly for her body.

Cayapó (highlands of Brazil)

Opossum

Ombú

bushy-tailed Olingo

Why the Opossum's Tail Is Bald

Opossum used to have a big fluffy tail. He was very vain about it and would parade about singing to it lovingly. The other animals found this behavior annoying.

One day Cricket offered to comb Opossum's tail, saying it would look especially beautiful for the big animal meeting that was coming up.

As Cricket brushed and combed, she sang a soothing song, and Opossum dozed off, dreaming of a string of animal admirers. When he woke up, Cricket was binding his tail. "Keep this cord on until the very last moment, and then surprise everybody with your amazing tail," she told him.

The next day Opossum strutted to his seat at the meeting, his tail still bound. Before sitting down, he dramatically unwound the cord and turned to see the animals' reaction.

Instead of gasps of admiration, he heard laughter! Opossum spun around. His tail was completely bald! Cricket had snipped off all his beautiful hair while he was asleep. Opossum was so ashamed that he could only turn over on his back with a silly look on his face.

Today, Opossum's descendants have bald, scaly tails, not like the long, luxurious one of their great-great-great-great-grandfather.

Cherokee (formerly North Carolina, Georgia, Alabama, and Tennessee; later Oklahoma)

P

Peccary

Piranha

Puma

The Boy and His Peccary Brother

The moon was a woman who had three sons. One day the two older boys climbed a tree and sat in it, eating fruit and ignoring their little brother. When he asked for fruit, they tossed him some half-chewed pulp. The boy took the pulp and molded it into a little gopher, which he buried under the tree. The gopher came alive and gnawed the tree's roots until it came crashing down, with the older brothers in it.

The little boy ran home, got some fresh tortillas from his mother, the moon, and raced back to the tree, where his brothers were still moaning and rubbing their knees and elbows. He shaped the tortillas into pig ears and snouts and stuck them to his brothers' faces, and they became pigs!

Wanting to take the pig-brothers home to his mother, the boy tried to grab their tails. One of them escaped and became the first pig. The other one's tail broke off in the boy's hand, and *that* pig-brother ran away to the mountains and became the first peccary.

"Where are your brothers?" asked the moon when the boy got home.

"Oh," he answered, "they must be off in the forest having fun." But the two older boys never returned, and the moon cried so much that she is pale, and her light is faint.

The youngest boy became the sun. If he hadn't made his brothers into animals, there would be three suns today. But no peccaries, and no pigs.

Tzotzil Maya (southern Mexico)

Pumpkins from Elk Hairs

When the Osage people came down from the sky to live on earth, the land was all covered with water. They couldn't go back to the sky, and they couldn't live in water, so they floated in the air, feeling very sad.

Then the elk, who was one of the people, called out to the winds for help. They blew so hard that the water turned into a mist, and rocks appeared. Now people could walk around, but still no plants could grow.

Gradually the water went down, and a little patch of soft, muddy earth appeared. This made the elk so happy that it rolled in the dirt, kicking up its heels with joy the way hoofed animals like to.

All of the elk's loose hairs stuck in the soft earth. They grew into plants, and soon there were pumpkins, potatoes, corn, beans, and all the other vegetables, trees, grains, and flowers.

Pumpkin

Osage (formerly Missouri, Arkansas, Kansas, and Oklahoma; later Oklahoma)

Why the Quetzal Is the Most Beautiful Bird

There was once a terrible fire that threatened to burn up the whole earth. If the seeds of corn and all the other crops weren't rescued, everyone would starve. But the fire was so hot that no one dared to get close.

Then a little mud-colored bird offered timidly, "I will save the seeds." At first everybody laughed. But when the tiny bird plunged head first into the raging flames, they stared in amazement.

First the bird dove into the hottest part of the fire and saved the corn; then the beans, tomatoes, and all the other crops. When he returned, featherless and blistered, the spirits rewarded him.

"From now on," they said, "you will be the most beautiful of all the birds. Your chest and throat will wear the color of fire. Your beak will be as yellow as ripe corn. And your tail feathers will flow and shine like its leaves."

And, before everyone's eyes, the little brown bird became the beautiful quetzal, the sacred bird of the Maya.

Maya (southern Mexico)

R

Raven

Raccoon

Rhea

The Raven and the Loon

In the far north, near Repulse Bay, the raven and the loon were in an igloo, decorating each other with tattoos. First the raven tattooed the loon with intricate black-and-white patterns. Then they changed places. But the loon didn't get very far in tattooing the raven, who kept jumping up and shouting *ouch!*

Each time, the loon warned, "If you don't stop that right now, I'm going to get angry. . . ."

At last the raven's jumping was too much for the loon, who grabbed the drip pot from under the oil lamp and poured it over the raven's head. That is why ravens are black.

"Ouch! Ouch! Ouch!" shouted the raven, and hurled the oil lamp at the loon, who had almost gotten out the door, and broke both of its legs. And that is why loons can't walk very well.

Repulse Bay Eskimo (northeastern Canada)

Skunk Sunflower

Sloth

Salmon

The Skunk in Love with the Moon

Añathuya, the skunk, fell in love with Pajsi, the moon. All night long, with tears in his eyes, he watched her move across the sky. The other animals wanted to help him reach his love, but none could fly or climb that high. Except, perhaps, for Mallku, the terrifying condor.

A few brave animals went to the condor and begged him to help their friend. "No way!" growled Mallku at first. "That skunk stinks!" But at last he said yes. With the lovesick skunk on his back, he soared into the sky.

The thin air made Añathuya feel dizzy and weak. Even the condor was tiring by the time they reached the moon. Añathuya kissed Pajsi's cheek, but the air was too thin for the skunk and the condor, and soon they had to return to earth.

In time, Añathuya got over his passion for the moon, but you can still see the smudges where the skunk kissed her with his dirty little nose.

Aymara (Bolivia)

Tapir

Tomato

Turkey

The First Tapir

After the animals were swept away in a great flood, the surviving Kaingang people had to carve new ones out of wood. First they carved a jaguar. Using ashes, they painted it with spots. When it was finished, they said, "You are a jaguar, and you will eat animals." The jaguar ran off into the forest, and it has eaten animals ever since.

Then the people carved a tapir, but they were a bit tired, so its shape was a little strange; and there were no more ashes left, so it didn't have any spots. When they were finished, they said, "You are a tapir, and you will eat animals."

But the people hadn't formed the tapir's ears very well. "*What* will I eat?" it asked.

By now the people were busy thinking about what to carve next, and they shouted in the tapir's ear: *"You will eat leaves and branches!"* And so, because of the people's impatience, tapirs eat prickly branches and brambles that no other animals will touch.

Kaingang (Brazil and northeastern Argentina)

Tobacco

Galápagos Tortoise

Toucan

The First Tobacco

A long, long time ago, there were some Kogi people who loved to listen to stories. They would gather around outside a house where somebody was telling one. Often the storytelling went on all night long, and when dawn arrived, the listeners were still there, their ears pressed up against the walls of the houses, looking almost as though they were rooted to the earth.

After a while they really did grow roots. The Great Mother turned them into tobacco plants, which the Kogi plant right up against the walls of their houses. So now the tobacco people can listen to stories whenever they are being told inside.

Kogi (Colombia)

U

white Uakari

Umbrella bird

Upland cotton

The Sloth and the White Uakari Monkey

The people told the sloth and the white uakari monkey to climb a tree. The monkey scampered up in a few seconds, but the sloth climbed very, very slowly. When the monkey reached the top of the tree, it asked, "Now what?"

"Now stay where you are," said the people. "Wait for the sloth."

But the sloth had not even reached the first branch. "Is this high enough?" it asked.

"No, keep climbing!" said the people.

Meanwhile, the monkey was running up and down the tree. "I'm bored!" it said. Finally the sloth stopped climbing. It hung upside down from a branch and nobody could get it to budge.

"You two are impossible!" said the people. "One won't move; the other won't keep still!"

And that's how it is today: sloths hang upside down, not moving, and uakari monkeys swing from branch to branch. And neither likes to come down to the ground. They have lived in the trees ever since the people told them to climb.

Yanomamo (Brazil and Venezuela)

Viscacha

Vanilla

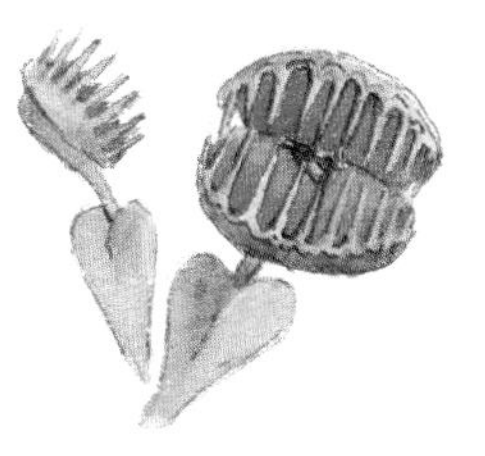

Venus's-flytrap

The Fox and the Viscachas

Two viscachas found two scraps of cloth. "A blanket for each of us!" they said. But the scraps were too small even for viscachas.

The little rodents decided to sew the pieces together to make one big blanket for both of them. "But where can we find a needle and thread?" they asked.

Just then a fox came by. "You can borrow my needle and thread if I can share your blanket." The viscachas agreed, and sat down to sew.

That evening a chilly wind blew. "Let's try our blanket," said the fox. "You each contributed a scrap of cloth, and I brought the thread, right?"

"That's right," said the viscachas.

"And so I will lie under my part," said the fox. The viscachas nodded. "Which is in the middle," said the fox. The viscachas nodded again. So the fox lay down in the middle, warm and cozy, while the viscachas shivered on the outside.

As usual, the fox had gotten the better of the deal. Poor viscachas!

Argentine pampas

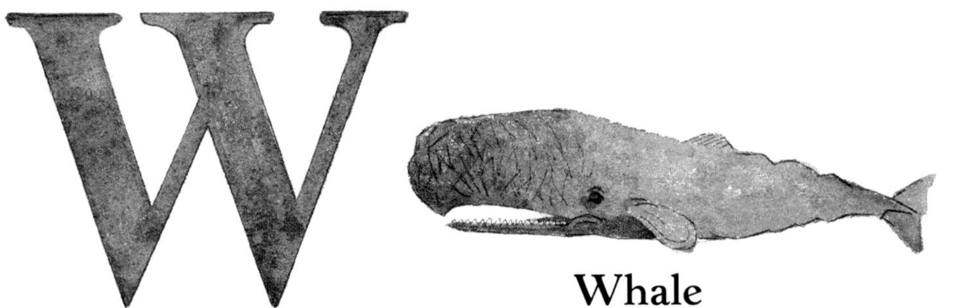

Why the Whale Lives in the Ocean

There was a time when the whale had short, stubby legs and lived on land. It was always swallowing people, animals, trees, even whole towns. And nobody knew what was happening to them.

Then Elal, the creator, saw the whale swallow a herd of guanacos. "So that's it!" he thought.

He turned himself into a deerfly and flew into the whale's mouth. Inside, he saw trees, houses, animals, and a lot of bored, homesick people. Elal, the deerfly, tickled the whale's belly button. Then he tickled its huge heart, and the whale sighed. "I'm going to cut this monster open with a knife," Elal said loudly.

"Hah!" shouted the whale. *"Hah! HAH!"* And all the people and animals and trees and towns came flying out of its mouth.

When he was outside, Elal spoke sternly to the whale. "There's been enough swallowing!" he said. "You'd better go live in the ocean!"

So the whale waddled down to the shore. Its feet soon turned into flippers, and now no one remembers that whales used to live on land. Some people even think whales are fish!

Aonik'enk (southern Argentina)

Xenosaurus

Xenops

Xenosaurus: Happy Lizard

The Aztecs divided the year into eighteen months. Each month had twenty days. The days had names, such as Flower, Water, Jaguar, or Flint Knife, and people's fortunes depended on their birthdays. People who were born on the day of the House, for example, liked to stay at home, while a person born under the sign of the Deer preferred to roam through the woods.

The fourth day of the month was called Lizard. How would life be for a person born on that day?

Think of the Mexican xenosaurus. It stays quietly hiding among leaves and roots, and the termites and ants it likes to eat seem to fly right into its mouth. Often it spends the day half-submerged in the water, perfectly still except for its eyes, which scan the area for insects foolish enough to come into its territory.

In the same way, people born under the sign of the lizard were never supposed to be poor or hungry. They would have plenty of everything they needed without doing much work. Perhaps they would be like the xenosaurus, happy in their bathtubs as riches flowed into their lives.

Aztec (Mexico)

Star Girl Brings Yuca from the Sky

One night a boy gazed up at a beautiful star. "I wish that star would fly down to me!" he said. "I'd marry her!" To his surprise, the star flew down and landed in his hand.

The boy hid the star inside a gourd. His mother was curious, and one day she opened the gourd. Out stepped the star, who became a girl. The boy and the girl got married.

The star girl missed the foods she had eaten in the sky. On earth, people hunted animals, but there weren't any food plants. "Let's go up and visit my old home," she said to her husband. "We can fly there." But the idea of flying through space frightened the boy, so she went alone. She clung to a little tree, and her husband pulled it way back, like a slingshot, and—*zoom!*—she flew into the sky.

When she returned, she brought yuca and sweet potatoes and many other plants. The girl and the boy planted them, and they were ready to eat the next day. Growing food was easy, and they lived very happily.

But not happily ever after. One day they had a fight, and the star girl returned to the sky. She left behind the yuca and other plants, but now they no longer ripen in one day. Now they take weeks or months to ripen, and people have to work hard preparing them, too.

Cayapó (highlands of Brazil)

Zebra swallowtail butterfly

Zinnia

Zompopo

Zompopos in the Garden

In an old, old book called the *Popol Vuh,* there is the story of two boys who played the ancient ball game against the Lords of the Underworld. The boys lost, and so they had to bring the Lords four gourds filled with the petals of a special kind of flower that grew only in the Lords' own flower gardens. By early the next morning, they had to have a gourd of red petals, one of yellow, one of white, and one of all three colors together.

The garden was protected by night birds, and the task appeared impossible.

The boys called the zompopos, the leaf-cutter ants, to ask for help. The guards sat on branches, turning their heads back and forth. They didn't notice the ants swarming into the garden, cutting and carrying away loads of flowers. They just sat there with their mouths open, even when the zompopos nibbled at their tails and wings.

By dawn, when the Lords of the Underworld returned, there were four gourds of flower petals waiting for them.

The lords punished their guards by tearing open their beaks, which is why the mouths of those birds—chuck-will's-widows—are split today.

And that is how, with the help of the zompopos, the two boys were able to pass the test. They had to perform many more feats, even more difficult than this one. But that, as they say, is another story, a very long and very, very old one. . . .

Quiché Maya (Guatemala)

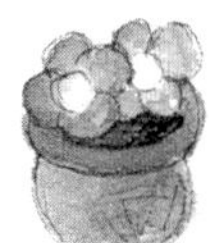

Notes on the Stories

"The Anteater: Origin of the Dance" is based on a story of the Guaraní, whose language is widely spoken in Paraguay and in parts of Brazil and Argentina.

"How the Armadillo Got Its Armor." The three-banded armadillo of this folktale from northwestern Argentina is the only one that rolls up into a ball.

"The Beans" combines details from a few of the many stories of rain dwarfs, angels, or spirits told in Guatemala and southern Mexico.

"Coyote and the Origin of Death" comes from a Caddo story. Coyote is an important figure in North American mythology, often making bad things happen.

"Corn and Chocolate" is from an ancient Aztec myth about the origin of corn, or maize. People first cultivated corn in Mexico thousands of years before the Aztecs. Cacao, too, was important: as well as drinking and eating it, the Aztecs used the beans as money.

"Big Duck and the Ducks" is part of a longer Seneca story in which Twentgowa keeps trying to learn food-getting magic, each time with ridiculous consequences.

"Where Emperor Penguins Come From" is based on myths of the Selk'nam, recently extinct, and of the Yamana, whose fishing canoes with fires on board inspired the name "Tierra del Fuego," or "land of fire."

"The Singing Fox" is one of a cycle of stories about Elal, the creator/hero of the Aonik'enk, or Tehuelches, very tall people of Patagonia.

"Grizzly Bear Gets Left Behind" is based on a short episode from a Sanpoil myth in which Beaver steals fire from the sky with the other animals' help.

"The Hummingbird and the Tapir" is retold from a story of the Yanomamo. A recent gold rush in their territory has brought disease, pollution, and massacre.

"The First Iguana" is from a story of the Cuiva, who are surrounded by many kinds of animals and often tell of human-animal transformations.

"When Jaguars Ate the Moon" is retold from several Toba accounts of a terrible fire. In many parts of the world, eclipses are attributed to ferocious animals that eat the moon.

"Kinkajou and the Food Tree." This is a much shortened version of a myth of the Cuiva, who also told the story "The First Iguana."

"The Lost Llama" is retold from a story of the Aymara, who inherited language and culture from the ancient Inca civilization.

"The Flood and the Howler Monkeys" is based on Yaruro mythology. Most New World monkeys have prehensile tails, making it possible for them to live in often flooded areas.

"The Moose and the Catfish" is retold from a story of the Menominee, who originally lived near the western Great Lakes and harvested wild rice from the marshes along their shores.

"The Nighthawk" is from a story of the Cayapó, who live in the highlands of Brazil. Many stories of the Americas tell of detached heads that cannot return to their bodies.

"Why the Opossum's Tail Is Bald" is from a Cherokee story, which would be told with songs (for example, when the opossum sings to his tail).

"The Boy and His Peccary Brother" is retold from a present-day Tzotzil Maya story. In ancient Mayan mythology, the older brothers become monkeys. Peccaries, but not pigs, are native to the Americas.

"Pumpkins from Elk Hairs" is retold from mythology of the Osage. Though farming was important to them, they also hunted buffalo at various times of year.

"Why the Quetzal Is the Most Beautiful Bird" is based on a Mexican story. "Quetzal" is the Aztec word from which comes the name of the god Quetzalcoatl.

"The Raven and the Loon" is retold from a Repulse Bay Eskimo story. Tattooing is a traditional form of decoration for many Eskimo and other northern peoples.

"The Skunk in Love with the Moon" is a folktale from Bolivia. A similar story, but with the fox as the protagonist, was told at the time of the Incas.

"The First Tapir" is based on a story of the Kaingang, who work together to hunt tapirs, peccaries, and other big game.

"The First Tobacco" is retold from a story of the Kogi of Colombia, who build special houses just for myth and storytelling.

"The Sloth and the White Uakari Monkey," like "The Hummingbird and the Tapir," is a retelling of a Yanomamo story. Uakaris are among the few New World monkeys with short tails.

"The Fox and the Viscachas" is a folktale of the Argentine pampas. Viscachas are rodents that collect all kinds of junk.

"Why the Whale Lives in the Ocean," like "The Singing Fox," is part of the Aonik'enk Elal cycle.

"Xenosaurus: Happy Lizard" is based on the ancient Aztec calendar.

"Star Girl Brings Yuca from the Sky" is from a story of the Cayapó, who told "The Nighthawk." Yuca is also called manioc or cassava.

"Zompopos in the Garden" is based on one short episode in the exploits of the hero twins Hunahpu and Xbalanque in the *Popol Vuh* of the ancient Quiché Maya.

Selected Bibliography

Ábalos, Jorge W. *Animales, leyendas y coplas,* 2nd ed. Buenos Aires: Editorial Losada, 1966.

Astrov, Margot. *American Indian Prose and Poetry, An Anthology.* New York: John Day Company, 1962. (Published in 1946 as *The Winged Serpent.*)

Bierhorst, John, ed. *The Hungry Woman: Myths and Legends of the Aztecs.* New York: William Morrow & Company, 1984.

———. *The Mythology of Mexico and Central America.* New York: William Morrow & Company, 1990.

Clark, Ella. *Indian Legends of the Pacific Northwest.* Berkeley: University of California Press, 1953.

Coluccio, Felix, and Marta I. Coluccio. *Diccionario folklórico argentino.* 7th ed. Buenos Aires: Editorial Plus Ultra, 1991.

Durán, Fray Diego. *Book of the Gods and Rites and the Ancient Calendar.* Translated by Fernando Horcasitas and Doris Heyden. Norman: University of Oklahoma Press, 1971.

Fauna argentina. Edited by Graciela Montes and Miguel Angel Palermo. Buenos Aires: Centro Editor de América Latina, 1983–86.

Gossen, Gary. *Chamulas in the World of the Sun: Time and Space in a Mayan Oral Tradition.* Cambridge: Harvard University Press, 1974.

Hoffman, Walter James. *The Menominee Indians.* 14th Annual Report of the Bureau of American Ethnology. Washington, DC, 1892–93.

Jagendorf, M. A., and R. S. Boggs. *The King of the Mountains: A Treasury of Latin American Folk Stories.* New York: Vanguard Press, 1960.

Kilpatrick, Jack F., and Anna G. Kilpatrick. *Friends of Thunder: Folktales of the Oklahoma Cherokees.* Dallas: Southern Methodist University Press, 1964.

Laughlin, Robert M. *Of Cabbages and Kings: Tales from the Zinacantán.* Smithsonian Contributions to Anthropology, No. 25. Washington, DC, 1977.

Metraux, Alfred. *Myths of the Toba and Pilagá Indians of the Gran Chaco.* Memoirs of the American Folklore Society, vol. 40, 1946.

Mooney, James. *Myths of the Cherokee.* Annual Report of the Bureau of American Ethnology. Washington, DC, 1902.

Norman, Howard, ed. *Northern Tales: Traditional Stories of Eskimo and Indian Peoples.* New York: Pantheon Books, 1990.

Paredes-Candia, Antonio. *Cuentos populares bolivianos.* La Paz: Libreria-Editorial Popular, 1984.

Parker, Arthur C. *Seneca Myths and Folk Tales.* Buffalo, NY: Buffalo Historical Society, 1923.

Reichel-Dolmatoff, Gerardo. *Los Kogi: Una tribu de la Sierra Nevada de Santa Marta, Colombia.* 2nd ed. Bogotá: Nueva Biblioteca Colombiana de Cultura, 1985.

Sahagún, Bernardino de. *General History of the Things of New Spain (Florentine Codex).* Translated by Arthur J. O. Anderson and Charles E. Dribble. Sante Fe, NM: School of American Research; and Salt Lake City: University of Utah, 1950–82.

Siffredi, Alejandra. 1968. El ciclo de Elal, hérоe mítico de los aonik'enk. *Runa,* vol. XI.

Siffredi, Alejandra, and Marcelo Bormida. 1969–70. Mitología de los tehuelches meridionales. *Runa,* vol. XII.

Tedlock, Dennis. *Popol Vuh: The Definitive Edition of the Mayan Book of the Dawn of Life.* New York: Simon & Schuster, 1985.

Vidal de Battini, Berta E. *Cuentos y leyendas populares de la Argentina.* Vols. 1–3. Buenos Aires: Ediciones culturales argentinas, 1980.

Wilbert, Johannes, and Karin Simoneau, eds. *Folk Literature of the Cuiva Indians.* Los Angeles: UCLA Latin American Center Publications, University of California, 1991.

———. *Folk Literature of the Yanomamo Indians.* Los Angeles: UCLA Latin American Center Publications, University of California, 1990.

———. *Folk Literature of the Yaruro Indians.* Los Angeles: UCLA Latin American Center Publications, University of California, 1990.